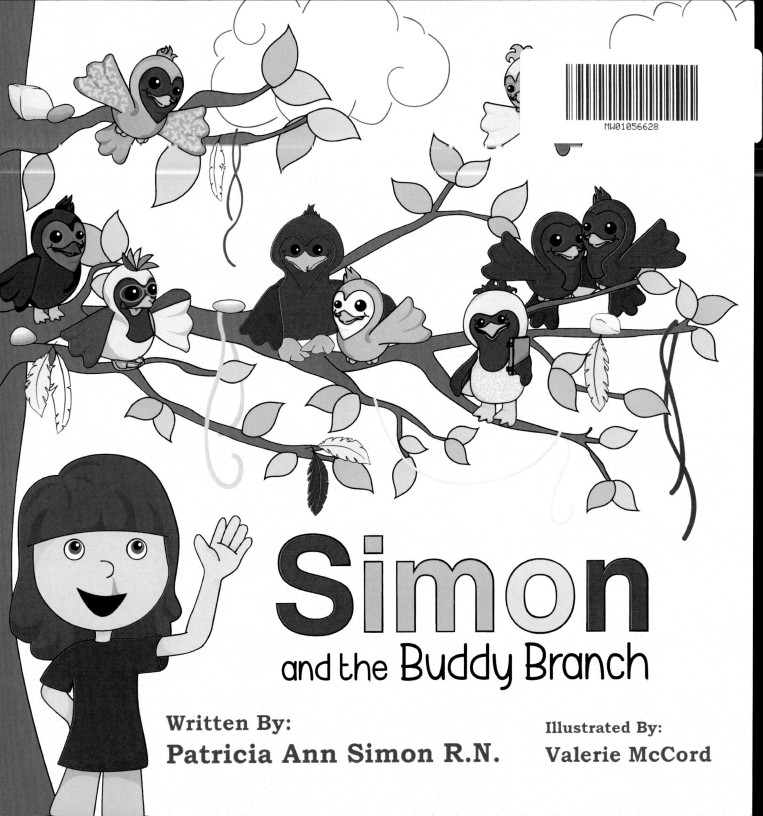

Simon
and the Buddy Branch

Written By:
Patricia Ann Simon R.N.

Illustrated By:
Valerie McCord

ISBN: 978-0-9988786-2-1 (sc)
ISBN: 978-0-9988786-3-8 (e)

Library of Congress Control Number: 2017905906
Because of the dynamic nature of the Internet, any web addresses or links contained in this
book may have changed since publication and may no longer be valid. The views expressed
in this work are solely those of the author and do not necessarily reflect the views of the
publisher, and the publisher hereby disclaims any responsibility for them.

Any people depicted in stock imagery provided by iStock are models,
and such images are being used for illustrative purposes only.
Certain stock imagery © iStock.
Rev date: 03/2020

We all have the name Buddy.
Extend your hand to others, and be kind.
We are different.
We are beautiful.
Your badge of courage makes you strong.

FOREWORD

Writing a book addressed to very young children requires special skills and talent.

Writing a children's book for children born with facial differences, based on personal experience, requires not only skills and talent, but also courage.

Patricia Simon was able to write two colorful books, *Smile with Simon* and *Simon and the Buddy Branch,* in an effort to educate children, parents, and educators dealing with children born with facial differences.

The message is simple but also very powerful: be tolerant and embrace children born with facial differences. Be supportive because they are wonderful human beings and deserve warm acceptance, not exclusion.

There is a message for the children born with facial differences as well: be brave—you are great kids, and with the support of your doctors, family, and community, you will have a successful future.

I spent my entire career treating patients born with facial differences, and I want to congratulate Patricia Simon for this beautiful initiative.

As a patient of mine said once, "It does not matter how you look outside but how you feel inside!"

This patient, Natalie, is about to graduate from college and enter the workforce with a big smile.

Thanks, Patricia!

Mimis Cohen MD, FACS, FAAP
Professor and Chief Division of
Plastic, Reconstruction and Cosmetic Surgery
University of Illinois, Chicago
Director Craniofacial Center UIC

Meet Simon, the cardinal.

Simon's nickname is **Smiling Simon**
because he loves to smile.

When Simon was small, he
hatched from his shell
with a gap in his beak.

The gap made it hard for
Simon to eat or smile.

Luckily, Simon met some friends who
helped him get his beak repaired.

This made Simon so happy
that his feathers turned a bright, joyful red,
and he has been smiling ever since.

One day, while taking a rest in an oak tree, Simon noticed a little blue jay sitting alone on a branch. **He was rocking back and forth, flapping his wings.**

At first, Simon thought the bird was hungry.
He grabbed a seed and flew over to him.

"Hello!" Simon chirped
in a friendly voice

"My name is Simon.
Would you like
something to eat?"

The little blue jay didn't seem to notice Simon or the
seed. He just looked at the ground, flapped his wings,
and rocked back and forth.

Simon thought long
and hard before asking,
"What's your name?"

For many seconds the little
blue jay said nothing. Then he
whispered, **"Buddy."**

"Nice to meet you, Buddy!"
Simon smiled. "How are you today?"

Simon waited patiently for the blue jay to answer.

Finally, Buddy chirped,
**"Bad day, bad day,
bad day."**

"Oh no," Simon said.
"What happened?"

Buddy rocked and flapped his wings for a long time.

**"No one came to
my birthday party,"**
he sadly peeped.

"But birds love birthday parties," Simon said.

"I was so excited," Buddy chirped.
"My parents sent tweets and decorated our nest."

"That's wonderful," said Simon.
"Why didn't the birds come?"

Buddy rocked and rocked and flapped his
wings. **"Because I'm different."**

Hearing Buddy's words made Simon sad.
"It's okay to be different.
I'm different too."

"But you have bright-red wings and a wonderful smile," Buddy said.

"True," said Simon, **"but my beak is different. See?"**
He leaned close so Buddy could see the stitches on his beak.

**"We may not be the same, but if we were,
it'd be a shame."** Buddy sighed and looked at the ground.

"Hey, I have an idea," Simon said.
"Let's visit my friend Patty. She's different too.
Come on, let's fly!"

Simon and Buddy flew to where Patty was
reading a book under her favorite redbud tree.
Simon chirped, **"Hello, Patty!"**

"Hi, Simon!" Patty looked up and Buddy
noticed the small scar above her lip.
"Who's your friend?"

"This is my new friend Buddy."
Simon replied.
"Buddy, this is Patty."

Patty could see Simon's new friend was different. She sat very still and waited for Buddy to relax.

"Would you like to hear the story of how I met Simon?" Patty asked.

After many minutes of flapping his wings and rocking back and forth, Buddy finally peeped, **"Yes, please."**

While Patty told Simon's story, the cardinal flew from tree to tree, inviting all the birds he knew to come to a birthday party for Buddy.

"Come on, Jose and Coco!
Come on, everyone!" Simon called.

**"Come help sing happy birthday to
my new friend, Buddy."**

It wasn't long before all of Simon's friends began landing on the branches around Buddy, from Jose, the wise crow, to Coco, the storytelling robin.

"Oh, look!" Patty smiled and clapped her hands. "Simon invited his friends to meet you."

When all the birds had arrived, Simon called for quiet, then said,

"Let's sing happy birthday to my new friend, Buddy."

The sound of the birds singing made Buddy so happy that his dull-blue feathers began to turn bright blue, and he forgot all about being different.

When they were done singing,
he flapped his stunning blue wings and chirped,
"Thank you!" again and again.

"I have an idea," said Simon. **"Let's call this branch, the Buddy Branch."**

"What's a buddy branch?" asked Buddy.

"A buddy is a friend like you," Simon explained. **"The Buddy Branch will be a special place for birds to meet and make friends.** If you are ever feeling alone, just sit on this branch. Another bird will see and join you. Lean on him or her in times of need. Friends help lift you up. What do you think?"

"Good idea!" the birds agreed, tweeting their approval.

"Let's decorate the branch to make it look special," Patty said.

All the birds liked this idea and flew off to find decorations.

Soon there were feathers, leaves, bits of string, and even some pretty colored pebbles that Patty had gathered.

In no time at all, **the Buddy Branch looked very special indeed.**

"I don't mind being different now," Buddy
chirped as he looked at his new friends, sitting on
the branch they'd named after him.

Buddy sang, "I am different, but I am beautiful."
The other birds joined in, singing,
"We are different, but we are beautiful."

And that's how Buddy made more friends than he could count and learned **it was okay to be different after all.**

SIMON'S FAVORITES

AboutFace.ca
ACPA American Cleft Palate-Craniofacial Association
Bear Necessities Pediatric Cancer Foundation
Beauty with a Twist
BORN A HERO, Pfeiffer's Health and Social Issues Awareness
Camp About Face
Cary Kanno-Musical Artist
Children's Craniofacial Association (CCA Kids)
CleftProud
Cuddles For Clefts
Doctors Without Borders
Emory Cleft Project-Dept Human Genetics, Emory Univ School of Medicine
Face the Future Foundation Illinois
FACES: The National Craniofacial Association
Facing Forward Inc
Love Me Love My Face: Jono Lancaster
MyFace
National Organization for Rare Disorders (NORD)
Noordhoff Craniofacial Foundation Philippines, Inc
Operation of Hope Worldwide
Operation Smile
Patients Rising
Pete's Diary: Peter Dankelson. Motivational Speaker
Rare Disease Legislative Advocates (RDLA)
Joe Rutland -CleftThoughts
Smile Train
Solidarity Bridge.org
St. Jude Children's Research Hospital
UI Health Craniofacial Center at the UIC College of Medicine

ABOUT PATRICIA ANN SIMON

I am a RN and was born with a cleft lip and palate.

I have written four books, *Smile with Simon, Simon and the Buddy Branch, Simon and Patty Go To Camp,* and *Simon and the Bully.* These children's books resonate with young people suffering from similar craniofacial differences.

My first children's book, *Smile with Simon* is about a cardinal named Simon, who's born with a gap in his beak. His gap made it difficult for him to eat, smile, and sing. In the story, he meets a young girl named Patty, who relates with Simon because she has a cleft lip.

I wrote a second book, *Simon and the Buddy Branch,* which further stresses the importance of kindness, love, and acceptance in the lives of children with facial differences.

My aim is to help children born with facial differences understand that it's okay to be different. I want to remind them that they are beautiful.

I am also a member of American Cleft Palate-Craniofacial Association (ACPA), Children's Craniofacial Association (CCA), Cleft Community Advisory Council (CCAC) for Smile Train, and former board member of Face the Future Foundation, which supports the efforts of University of Illinois Health Craniofacial Center.

I have given a keynote speech for the Inaugural Cleft Lip and Palate Team Day at Morgan Stanley Children's Hospital in New York Presbyterian Hospital,

My book, *Smile with Simon* was translated to Tagalog so that it could be used at a Philippine speech camp.

I created a webpage, www.smilewithsimon.org which features videos and songs that reinforce the message we are all different, and to be accepting and kind.

Books can be purchased directly through my website:
www.smilewithsimon.org